THIS NOTEBOOK BELONGS TO:

Iggy

THE QUESTIONEERS

IGGY PECK

AND THE MYSTERIOUS MANSION

by Andrea "Ghost Cat" Beaty

illustrations by David Roberts

AMULET BOOKS
NEW YORK

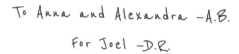

To Anna and Alexandra —A.B.

For Joel —D.R.

Cataloging-in-Publication Data has been applied for and may be obtained from the Library of Congress.

ISBN 978-1-4197-3692-6

Text copyright © 2020 Andrea Beaty
Illustrations copyright © 2020 David Roberts
Book design by Marcie Lawrence

Printed and bound in USA
10 9 8 7 6 5 4 3 2 1

Amulet Books are available at special discounts when purchased in quantity for premiums and promotions as well as fundraising or educational use. Special editions can also be created to specification. For details, contact specialsales@abramsbooks.com or the address below.

ABRAMS The Art of Books
195 Broadway, New York, NY 10007
abramsbooks.com

CHAPTER I

Iggy Peck sat on a log and studied the giant oak towering above him. A chilly wind rattled the golden leaves and sent them tumbling, one by one, onto the forest floor. Iggy's cat, Bricks, chased the leaves with a loud MEOW.

Iggy did not notice. He was busy designing a treehouse. Iggy Peck was an architect and he designed houses everywhere he went, even the forest.

"This oak is perfect for a Victorian mansion," said Iggy.

"Ooh!" said Iggy. "That elm tree needs a cottage and that maple needs a bungalow! Or a castle!"

Iggy unclipped his paper and flipped it over. Before he could clip it down again— *WHOOSH!*—the wind ripped the paper from his hand and sent it flying through the forest.

"Hey!" cried Iggy.

"Meow!" cried Bricks.

Iggy and Bricks scrambled after the paper, which tumbled deeper and deeper into the dim woods.

WHACK!

Iggy's sneaker hit a root and he tripped. The clipboard flew out of his hand as Iggy stumbled and tumbled head over heels down . . . down . . . down the hill.

"Whooooaaaaaaa-whooooaaaaa!" he yelled.

Iggy slammed into something very hard beneath the leaves. He sat up and rubbed his shoulder.

"Ouch!" he said.

Bricks hissed.

"What's wro—?" Iggy started.

Suddenly, a strong gust of wind blew away the leaves and revealed what Iggy had hit.

"Whoa," he said, staring into a pair of stone-cold eyes.

Three White Marxble
CATS

WHIMSY   HAPPINESS   WONDER

(a bit like Bricks)

CHAPTER 2

The eyes stared back at Iggy from the face of a white marble cat with the word HAPPINESS carved into its base. It stood beside two other stone cats. One titled WHIMSY and the other, WONDER. Iggy touched the cool stone of the third cat.

"They look like you, Bricks!" he said.

Bricks hissed and arched his back.

Iggy laughed.

"Don't be scared!" he said. "They can't hurt—"

Iggy stopped short. A glimpse of something white caught his eye. A few feet behind the cats, a slab of vine-covered marble jutted from the forest floor. He stepped closer. Iggy reached through the vines and his fingers touched cold marble. His hand trembled as he pulled back the vines, revealing a weathered marble slab with faint letters: C. SHERBERT AND H. SHERBERT, 1918.

Iggy gasped.

"It's a gravestone," Iggy whispered.

Another gravestone stood to the left. It seemed newer, its lettering unmelted by time and rain. It simply read: PIERRE GLACE. Nearby, the remains of a small cottage stood like an ancient ruin. Long abandoned. Long forgotten.

Bricks hissed again and bristled his fur. Iggy nodded.

"It is spooky," he said, picking up Bricks. "Let's get home."

Iggy looked around. It was much darker now. The wind was chillier and stronger. A storm was brewing.

He had lost track of time. He always did when he was thinking about architecture—which was all the time. But he couldn't help it. Thinking about architecture always made Iggy feel like he was doing exactly what he should be doing. Even when he was supposed to be doing something else. Sometimes, it got him in trouble. He was pretty sure that this was going to be one of those times. He wasn't supposed to go past the edge of the woods, and he should have been home long ago.

"C'mon, Bricks," he said. "We'd better—"

Suddenly, a flash of lightning lit up the forest.

BAM!—a crack of thunder split the air.

Bricks squirmed out of Iggy's arms and bolted through the trees.

"Bricks!" yelled Iggy, chasing after him.

BOOM! CRASH!

MEOW!

Bricks zigged and zagged through the trees, changing direction with each lightning flash and thunder crash.

MEOW!

"Come back!" Iggy yelled.

Iggy chased Bricks deeper and deeper into the woods. At last, Bricks dived into the end of a hollow log and hunkered down, trembling in the storm. Iggy caught up and knelt beside the log.

"It's okay, Bricks," he said. "It's okay."

Iggy reached into the log and pulled out the shivering cat. He clutched Bricks close and looked around.

"Where are we?" he asked.

Nothing looked familiar.

"Which way do we go?" he wondered.

CREEEAAAAK!

Iggy looked up as a large, dead branch swayed

in the wind and—*CRACK!*—Iggy jumped out of the way just as the limb crashed onto the hollow log, smashing it to smithereens.

"That was too close," said Iggy. "Let's get out of here!"

Iggy ran.

PLOP! PLOP! PLOP!

Large raindrops splattered onto his face. In moments, it was pouring. Iggy stumbled through the darkening woods until, at last, he saw a gap in the trees.

"It's a path!" he said.

Iggy ran down the uneven path, which opened onto a wide, overgrown lawn. A brilliant flash of lightning revealed the outline of an enormous dark house, and suddenly Iggy Peck knew exactly where he was.

"Uh-oh," he whispered, and pulled Bricks a little closer.

Iggy looked at the looming, shadowy building

before him. He took a deep breath and stepped onto the lawn.

"Architects are brave," Iggy whispered. "Architects are brave . . ."

At that moment, Iggy did not feel brave. Bricks growled.

"Architects and their cats are brave," Iggy whispered.

A streak of lightning sliced across the sky. Iggy took a deep breath and ran toward the Mysterious Mansion.

I ♥ Gothic Architecture

Gothic castles in Movies are always ⚡ HAUNTED ⚡

Do ghosts use stairs?

Gothic Architecture

- Originated in -
- 12th Century -
FRANCE

Ooooh La La

CHAPTER 3

Bricks jumped from Iggy's arms onto the weatherworn porch and shook his fur, spraying Iggy with water. Iggy looked around nervously at the spooky house as the dark trees whipped furiously in the storm.

This was the Sherbert House, but everyone in Blue River Creek called it the Mysterious Mansion. It had been empty for longer than anyone could remember. But everyone knew the strange stories. Stories of the famous ice cream baron Herbert Sherbert, and his wife, Candace. They were very important in Blue River Creek's history. They'd built the Blue River Creek library, the original school, and the train station.

The stories said that she'd died young and he went away and was never seen again. Some said their ghosts haunted the house and played eerie music that filled the air. There were darker tales of a woman whose cries could be heard late at night if you dared to get close enough to the house to listen. They said the ghosts were looking for something—or someone!

They said that sometimes, on a dark and stormy night, you could even hear a voice calling.

"liiiiiiiiiiggy . . . liiiiiiiiiiiiiiiggyyyyyyyy . . ."

CHAPTER 4

Iggy froze. A croaking, creaking voice was calling his name!

His heart banged in his chest and he wanted to run, but his feet were like lead. He heard a footstep behind him.

"Iiiiiiiiiggy!"

Another footstep.

"Iiiiiiiiiiggy!"

It was right behind him. Iggy held his breath and closed his eyes.

"Iiiiiiiiiig—"

Suddenly, a hand grabbed his shoulder.

"EEEEEK!" yelled Iggy, jumping straight into the air.

He whirled around and came face-to-face with—

"Mrs. Twist?!" Iggy cried.

"Iiiiiiiiggyyy—" said the old woman, coughing into her elbow.

COUGH. COUGH.

"Ahem—" she said.

She stood up, cleared her throat again, and chuckled. It was Bernice Twist with her great-niece, Ada. Bernice owned the Can You Dig It? shop. It was filled with treasures from around Blue River Creek. She was the town historian, geologist, anthropologist, and paleontologist, all in one person. Her shop had everything from old buttons to dinosaur bones. If it could be dug from

the ground, she had it in her shop. It was one of Iggy's favorite places to go with his friends.

Aunt Bernice cleared her throat again.

"Phew! Oh my. Ahem," she said. "I'm so sorry, Iggy. I had a frog in my throat."

"Can I see?" asked Ada. "What kind of frog is it? How do you know it's not a toad? People often confuse them but it's easy to tell. Toads are covered with bumps. Are there bumps?"

"It's just a saying, Ada," said Aunt Bernice with a smile. "Not a real frog."

"Oh," said Ada. She was disappointed. "That's too bad. Why don't people say you have a turtle in your throat? Like a turtleneck? Why do people wear turtlenecks? You wear turtlenecks, Iggy! Why do you do that? Do you have bumps?"

Iggy relaxed. He was glad to see his friend Ada and her great-aunt Bernice.

CHAPTER 5

Finding yourself on the porch of a haunted house on a dark, stormy night was a lot less scary with friends. Even for a brave architect and his cat.

"I'm glad to see you!" said Iggy.

"Why are you out in this weather?" asked Aunt Bernice.

Iggy told them about designing treehouses and the graves by the run-down cottage in the woods.

"But why are *you* here?" Iggy asked.

Aunt Bernice pointed to the mansion.

"This is my shiny new house!" she said. "I got a letter with the surprising news today! And this key!"

She held up a very old key on a frayed ribbon.

Though it was dark, Iggy could tell that there was nothing new or shiny about the house. In fact, it was very, very old. The porch was worn and had not been painted for many years.

"You own the Mysterious Mansion?" asked Iggy. "They say it's haunted!"

"People say a lot of things," said Aunt Bernice.

"We should do an experiment to see if it is!" said Ada, who loved experiments.

"If it is," said Iggy, "I could design a new house for the ghost. Do ghosts use stairs? Or doors? Closets? Do they like modern architecture? I bet they like Gothic architecture. Gothic castles in movies are always haunted. But that's just the movies."

Aunt Bernice chuckled. She loved Ada and her friends. They were full of questions. That's why she had given the group their nickname: the Questioneers.

Aunt Bernice thought for a moment.

"Well," she said. "I never thought I'd be standing on this spot again."

"You've been here before?" asked Ada.

"Of course," said Aunt Bernice. "The last time was during the war, and I was a very young woman. Agnes Lu came with me to collect junk for the war effort. The country needed metal and rubber to make jeeps and planes. The old Frenchman who took care of the place met us right here in the yard with a wagonful of stuff."

"Pierre Glace?" asked Iggy.

"Yes!" said Aunt Bernice. "He was the caretaker here, but he still had family in France, which was invaded during World War II, you know. Those were bad times.

"He donated some brass lamps and vases," she said. "And a beautiful copper weathervane shaped like an ice cream cone. It was the color of Herbert Sherbert's most famous flavor: Green Goose!"

"Blech!" said Iggy. "Goose-flavored ice cream?"

Aunt Bernice laughed.

"Gooseberry," she said. "It made him famous around the world. It was also very good. Too bad nobody makes that anymore.

"Okay," she said. "Enough chat. Let's go in!"

She handed the key to Ada, who tried to jam it into the lock.

"It's too big," said Ada.

Another flash of lightning lit the sky. Thunder growled through the forest.

"Hmm," said Aunt Bernice. "Let's come back when there's more light and less lightning! Ada, you may keep that key as a necklace. Iggy, we'll give you and Bricks a ride home. Your parents are probably wondering where you are."

"Can you come back tomorrow, Iggy?" asked Ada.

Iggy nodded. How could he pass up the chance to see inside the Mysterious Mansion? It might have ghosts. And even better, it had architecture!

The rain eased up for a moment, and they ran to Aunt Bernice's car. Bricks settled on the back seat between Ada and Iggy.

"I wonder what we'll find tomorrow," said Aunt Bernice as she started the car. "Maybe we'll find a quart of Green Goose ice cream! That would be a treat."

Gravel crackled beneath the tires as they drove down the tree-lined lane. Bricks purred and the rain gently drummed on the car roof as Iggy looked out the window.

Then, just as the mansion faded behind them, something caught his eye. At the edge of the wide wooden porch sat a small figure, as still as stone.

It was a white cat.

The car passed a tree and the view was blocked for a heartbeat. When the mansion briefly flickered into view once more, the cat was gone.

Iggy reached onto the car seat next to him. Bricks nuzzled his hand and purred as the lane turned once more and the mansion was lost, at last, in darkness.

To Mrs. Bernice Twist,

We are lawyers for the Estate of Mr. Herbert Sherbert, the world-famous creator of Green Goose ice cream.

Herbert Sherbet was a public figure, but a very private man. He believed that his wife's spirit remained in the house and he did not want anyone to disturb her. Since Mr. Sherbert did not have any heirs, his estate was handled by the caretaker, Monsieur Pierre Glace. Monsieur Glace died twenty-seven years ago. At that point, the Herbert mansion and money were placed in our care with two directions:

1. Use the money to pay taxes and care for the mansion.

2. When the money is gone, give the mansion to the person in Blue River Creek who has done the most to share the city's history with the public.

If anybody was to live in the house, Mr. Sherbert wanted it to be someone who loved Blue River Creek as much as he and Mrs. Sherbert had. We believe that you are that person.

The Can You Dig It? shop celebrates the history of Blue River Creek. It is filled with historical things dug up through the centuries. Of special interest is the display of archeological items from very, very old outhouses. Who knew that you could learn so much about people from what they threw away in outhouses? We did not. Nor did we care to.

Be that as it may, here is the deed and a key for the property at 1 Rocky Road, Blue River Creek. The property and contents, including original furnishings and art, are now yours.

Be well and best wishes,

Ms. Rachel Yabba, Esquire

Mr. George Dabba, Esquire

Mrs. Jane Dew, Esquire

Law Offices of Yabba, Dabba & Dew

P.S. Some say that the mansion is haunted. This is probably not true. Just in case:

The Law Offices of Yabba, Dabba & Dew are not responsible for the actions of ghosts or anything that causes shivers, nightmares, heebie-jeebies, or worse. Especially worse.

P.P.S. Contents have not been verified. As our property agent said after throwing the key into the river, "I'm not going in that haunted house. You go in there!"

We did not.

P.P.P.S. Ha-ha. Joke is on our property agent. Monsieur Glace gave us two keys. We are giving one to you. Please do not throw it in a river.

P.P.P.P.S. It is not funny that we just said "pee-pee" two times. Stop laughing.

P.P.P.P.P.S. We are retiring and moving to Fiji or maybe Iowa. Our office is now closed forever. The mansion is yours. No tag backs. No backsies. No returns.

P.P.P.P.P.P.S. Good luck.

P.P.P.P.P.P.P.S. You are going to need it.

CHAPTER 6

The next day was crisp, cool, and clear. The lawn of the Sherbert House was littered with leaves and branches that had snapped in the storm.

Iggy stood in front of the porch with Ada and Aunt Bernice. He looked around in awe.

"Wow," he said. "It's . . . It's . . ."

"It's beautiful," said Aunt Bernice. "It's one of a kind."

The building looked like a small mansion with a bunch of bigger mansions stuck to it.

"That original part is from the Victorian era," said Iggy. "But that part is Art Nouveau! They just kept adding on!"

"They didn't know when to stop!" said Aunt Bernice.

"Why would they?" asked Iggy. "It's very confusing. And marvelous. And I love it."

Aunt Bernice smiled.

"Have you ever met a house you didn't love?" she asked.

Iggy blushed.

Iggy was famous in Blue River Creek for his amazing architectural creations, including a stinky tower he'd made from diapers when he was only two. But his greatest creation was the bridge over the creek. He'd built it with his classmates when they'd gotten stuck on an island during a field trip with their teacher, Miss Lila Greer.

"What is Art Nouveau?" asked Ada.

"It's a style of architecture and art and design

that was really, really popular from about 1890 to 1910, but then got less popular over the next ten years. It had amazing, cool curves that were not symmetrical. And it had lots of leaves and flowers and other parts of nature. The people who made it wanted to look ahead to new styles instead of back to the Roman and Greek styles that were popular before. I made an Art Nouveau house in the lunchroom once," said Iggy. "Do you remember?"

"The carrot house?" asked Ada.

"No," said Iggy.

"The hot-dog house?" asked Ada.

Iggy shook his head.

"The PB&J house?" asked Ada. "The pizza house . . . meatballs . . . fish sticks?"

"No," said Iggy. "It was the curvy spaghetti house."

"Oh," said Ada. "You make a lot of food houses."

Iggy smiled proudly.

"I do," he said. "Don't I?"

Ada smiled.

"This house belonged to a very famous man," said Aunt Bernice. "Herbert Sherbert was famous for ice cream and even more for his musical pushcarts and train cars. He changed the ice cream business and traveled the world. Unfortunately, his wife, Candace, had terrible motion sickness and had to stay home."

"She couldn't travel the world with him?" asked Iggy. "She couldn't see the Eiffel Tower? Or the Parthenon? Or the Forbidden City? Or the Pyramids at Giza? Or the—"

"Or any of it," said Aunt Bernice. "But he brought it back for her. They say he created a room in this house for every place he went."

"Wow," said Iggy.

"He must have loved her so much," said Ada.

Aunt Bernice nodded.

"Herbert's heart broke when she died," said Aunt Bernice. "He shuttered up the house, left town, and nobody ever saw him again."

"Did he come back as a ghost?" asked Iggy.

"Let's find out," said Aunt Bernice, jingling a large ring of keys.

"The key from the lawyer didn't work, so I'm guessing it's for a door inside the house," she said. "But I've collected old keys in Blue River Creek for years. Maybe one will fit this door."

She flipped through the keys. Some were too big. Some were too small. At last, one fit. She turned the key.

CLICK.

CLICK.

CLUNK.

The lock clicked, but the door did not open.

"That's too bad," said Aunt Bernice.

Suddenly, there was a faint rumbling noise. It grew louder and louder and . . .

"What's that?" asked Iggy.

BUMP. BUMP. BUMP. BUMP.

The boards of the porch began to rise and fall like piano keys. A wave rolled from one end of the porch to the other and back again.

"The porch is moving!" yelled Ada.

"Whoa!" yelled Iggy. "I've never seen a house do that before! I like it!"

Aunt Bernice wobbled as the boards beneath her jumped.

The waves rolled faster and faster. Each wave was bigger than the last. Then, for a heartbeat, they stopped.

"Watch out!" yelled Ada.

Suddenly the boards began to crash up and down randomly. Iggy tried to run, but the boards tossed him back.

SMACK!

WHACK!

THWACK!

Suddenly, the board beneath Aunt Bernice's left foot rose up and sent her tumbling.

"Aunt Bernice!" yelled Ada.

Ada and Iggy grabbed Aunt Bernice's arms and the trio jumped clear of the porch. They landed in a heap on the overgrown lawn. Instantly, the boards stopped moving and there was silence.

A leaf skittered across the porch. Aunt Bernice, Iggy, and Ada looked at each other, too shocked to speak.

And that's when they heard it.

CLICK.

THUNK.

CRRREEEEEEEAAAAAAK . . .

Iggy's heart raced as the enormous wooden door of the Mysterious Mansion cracked open. Deep in the shadows, Iggy could see a dark figure moving toward them.

The figure moved closer. And closer.

Aunt Bernice, Ada, and Iggy hopped to their feet.

CREEEEEEAAAAAK.

The door swung open a little more and a little more and—

"Is that—?" asked Iggy.

"Can it be?" asked Aunt Bernice.

"But how—?" asked Ada.

A dim shaft of light flooded into the house through the open doorway. A hand reached into the light, then . . .

A full figure stepped into the doorway. It was—

Types of Doors

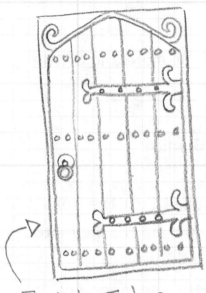

English Tudor

Neo-Classical-Revival

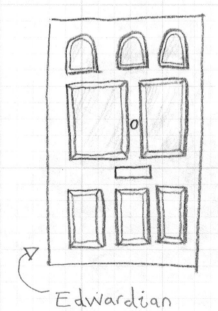

Edwardian

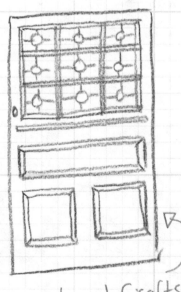

Arts and Crafts

CHAPTER 7

Sofia?!" said Iggy.

Sofia Valdez stepped into the light of the doorway and waved.

"Was that you banging on the door?" she asked.

Iggy, Ada, and Aunt Bernice did not answer. They stared at something behind Sofia. Something that was moving toward her from the deep shadows. It drew closer and closer and—

"Sofia!" said Iggy. "It's—"

"A really cool house!" said Sofia.

Closer . . . Closer . . .

"It's—" sputtered Iggy, pointing wildly behind Sofia.

"Awesome?" asked Sofia. "Wait until you see inside!"

"But . . . It's . . ." Iggy stammered.

"Creepy?" said Sofia. "Do you think it's haunted?"

"Sofia!" cried Aunt Bernice. "Get out of the house!"

"Why?" asked Sofia.

"Look out!" said Iggy.

A ghostly howl filled the darkness.

"Whooooooooooooo-WHOOOOOOOOO-WHOOOOOOOOOOOOOOO!"

Ada and Iggy jumped onto the porch and raced toward Sofia, but it was too late. Sofia whirled around just as the thing swooped around her and pulled her back into the shadows.

Art Nouveau

CHAPTER 8

S ofia!" yelled Ada.

Ada and Iggy raced through the doorway, tripped on the threshold, and toppled onto something that was very bumpy, very wiggly, and very giggly.

Aunt Bernice pushed the heavy door wide open and light flooded the entry hall.

Ada, Iggy, and Sofia were piled in a heap on top of a bumpy sheet.

"Hee-hee!" giggled a voice beneath the sheet.

"What do we have here?" asked Aunt Bernice. "A giggling ghost?"

Ada, Iggy, and Sofia scrambled to their feet, and Aunt Bernice snatched away the sheet to reveal a giggling girl in a red polka-dot bandana.

"Rosie!" said Iggy.

"Did I scare you?" asked Rosie. "I found this sheet on that chair."

"It was funny," said Sofia, breaking into a laugh.

Rosie, Ada, and Aunt Bernice couldn't help themselves, and soon, everyone was laughing. Everyone, that is, except Iggy Peck.

Iggy was too busy looking at the most beautiful room he had ever seen.

Happiness

is

the Key to

Everything!

CHAPTER 9

They stood in a grand entry hall with an iron and glass chandelier above them and a swirling mosaic tile floor below. At the center of the swirls were the words: HAPPINESS IS THE KEY TO EVERYTHING.

"Hey," said Aunt Bernice. "That was Herbert Sherbert's slogan. He put that on everything he built in Blue River Creek. The train station had that on the platform. In the rotunda of the old library. In the original school, there was a big painting of a Green Goose ice cream cone with those words around it. I don't think the teachers liked it, but we kids sure did. Especially on hot days."

"Herbert Sherbert really knew how to advertise!" said Sofia.

"And make ice cream," said Aunt Bernice. "Wish I had some now!"

A curved wrought-iron banister led to the second floor. The walls were covered with large murals of the history of Blue River Creek from the dinosaurs to the turn of the twentieth century.

"I can't believe this!" said Iggy. "The outside of this part of the house is Victorian-era and the inside is Art Nouveau! Those are my favorite styles of houses besides Gothic, Romanesque, and Modern, and—"

"I think that dinosaur is eating ice cream," said Sofia. "But it's too dark to tell."

Even with the door wide open, the room was dim.

"Look!" said Rosie. "A button!"

"That's an old light switch," said Aunt Bernice, "but it won't work. The wires are too old to handle modern electric service. This house would have been one of the first in Blue River Creek to be built for electricity."

"How will you live here without electricity, Aunt Bernice?" asked Ada.

Aunt Bernice sighed.

"I don't think I'll get to live here, Ada," said Aunt Bernice sadly. "It would cost a fortune to update this place. But the letter said there was furniture, so maybe I can sell some of it to pay for repairs."

She smiled hopefully.

"What's this lever?" asked Rosie Revere.

"Don't pull—" cried Aunt Bernice.

But it was too late.

THUNK! CLUNK! THUNK! CLUNK!

BAM! BAM! BAM!

The giant metal shutters covering the enormous windows flipped open and slammed against the outside of the house. Light streamed through the leaded glass windows of the Great Hall of the Mysterious Mansion.

"Wow!" said Iggy.

"Wow!" said Rosie.

"Wow!" said Sofia.

Ada did not say anything. She was thinking.

She tapped on her chin and looked at Sofia and Rosie.

"Wait a second," she said. "How did you get in here?"

"We climbed in through the kitchen window!" said Rosie.

"What?" asked Aunt Bernice.

"The storm blew a big tree through the kitchen window," said Sofia. "So we came through to let you in."

"How did you know we would be here?" asked Ada.

"Iggy's dad told my aunt and she told me," said Rosie. "So we came out to see if we could help, and we found the tree in the window!"

"Was there glass?" asked Aunt Bernice. "You could've been hurt!"

"It's all under the tree," said Rosie. "We just stayed on the branches."

"Ooooph," said Aunt Bernice. "Let's all be careful and stick togeth—"

It was too late. Iggy had already dashed up the grand staircase with the rest of the Questioneers on his heels. Aunt Bernice heard them open doors upstairs.

"Wow!" Iggy yelled. "Every room is like a different country!"

"Here's Egypt!" yelled Ada.

"Spain!" yelled Sofia.

"Italy!" yelled Iggy.

"Russia! . . . China! . . . Morocco! . . ."

Downstairs, Aunt Bernice looked quietly at the magnificent Great Hall of the Mysterious Mansion. The sun streamed through the enormous windows and lit the murals of happy times from Blue River Creek. Bernice smiled. She imagined the whole town gathered for parties in the mansion. But she couldn't help thinking about Herbert Sherbert. He would have been lonely in such a big house after Candace died. What happened to him then? Could those old stories be true? Did their ghosts haunt the Mysterious Mansion?

Perhaps it was a small breeze that blew in through the door or a passing cloud blocking the sun from the tall windows, but for a moment, Aunt Bernice felt a chill and shuddered. Then, the chill passed.

She looked around once more, then followed the Questioneers up the wide marble steps.

did
Dinosaurs
eat
ice cream
? ? ?

CHAPTER 10

Herbert Sherbert had indeed traveled far and wide. Each room upstairs was like visiting a different country. The walls were covered with colorful murals showing the scenery and landmarks and wildlife of the various lands, all in the Art Nouveau style, which Iggy loved. Like the murals in the Great Hall, each included someone eating ice cream.

What each room did not include was furniture. There were no beds, tables, chairs, or dressers.

Where was the furniture mentioned in the letter? Surely there had been furniture if Pierre Glace had donated brass lamps and vases from the house so long ago.

As Aunt Bernice toured the house, she grew sadder. Each room was more beautiful than the last. But without antiques to sell, there was no way she could keep the house.

She found the Questioneers in a room with a mural that had a lush tropical jungle with a tiger, a baby elephant, and other animals peeking from the vegetation on one end, and a royal palace with a golden roof on the other.

"That's the Grand Palace in Bangkok, Thailand!" said Iggy. "Though when it was made, the country was called Siam. Its architecture is very unique. Someday, I want to go there."

"Look, Iggy!" said Ada. "There's Bricks!"

A white cat with two different-colored eyes peeked from behind a pillar.

"Do you think that is Brick's ancestor?" she asked. "Why do they have different-colored eyes? I'm going to read about that when I get home."

Iggy did not answer. He was thinking about the cat statues in the graveyard. Was there a connection?

"Speaking of home," said Aunt Bernice, "it's time to wrap up this adventure."

They wandered back to the Great Hall, where the sunlight streamed through the large windows. It filled Iggy with joy. But Aunt Bernice smiled sadly. She looked at the single chair sitting before the fireplace and the large portrait hanging above the mantle. The painting was covered with a sheet.

"This chair and that painting are all that's left," she said. "I can't afford to replace the roof just by selling those."

"Let's look!" said Ada, tugging at the corner of the sheet.

The sheet tumbled to the ground, revealing a wedding portrait of an elegant couple. In one hand, the bride held a bouquet of jasmine. In the other, she held a white cat with two different-colored eyes. The couple smiled widely, but their eyes held a single emotion.

Sorrow.

"Why is the portrait crooked?" asked Ada, pushing up on the bottom corner of the frame.

"I wonder if the cat came from Thai—" Iggy started.

CRRREEEEEAAAAK . . .

A sudden sound cut him short.

A deep rumbling noise filled the air. It gave

way to a wheezing sound that changed into a strong, clear note. It was as if the house were humming. The sound grew louder and louder, and soon, a steady thump began from somewhere upstairs. There was a new note and then another and another. It was music! The house itself was playing a song.

Suddenly, the shutters on the Great Hall windows slammed shut. Almost as quickly, they flew open again. The shutters opened and shut in rhythm with the music. At first, the song was jolly, like a carnival ride, but then it twisted and became eerie and creepy.

The Questioneers looked at one another with wide eyes.

Suddenly, they heard a new sound rise above the music. It was a faint sound that sent chills up their spines.

It was an earsplitting yowl, like the sound of a woman crying.

CHAPTER 11

Then suddenly—

BAM! BAM! BAM!

The shutters slammed shut, leaving only the light from the open door.

CRRRREEEEEAAAAAK!

The massive front door of the mansion was closing!

"Get out!" yelled Iggy. "Hurry!"

Aunt Bernice and the Questioneers ran through the doorway.

BAM!

The giant door slammed shut behind them. The porch boards rose and fell beneath their feet.

"Watch out!" yelled Ada. "Get off the porch!"

They jumped off the porch. Instantly, the boards stopped moving, and there was silence.

Aunt Bernice, Iggy, Ada, Sofia, and Rosie stood silently in the leaf-covered grass in front of the Mysterious Mansion. Then, from the corner of his eye, Iggy saw a white blur as something darted around the side of the house.

"The white cat!" he yelled.

Iggy ran, but when he turned the corner, there was no white cat. Only a torn piece of paper snagged on a fallen branch. Iggy recognized the paper. He plucked his treehouse drawing from the branch, folded it neatly, and stuck it into his pocket.

CHAPTER 12

I'll get Bee and Beau to board up the window," Aunt Bernice said with a sigh as she dropped the kids off at Iggy's house. Bee and Beau ran a handyman business when they weren't working as the recyclers in town or volunteering at the fire department and the library.

Aunt Bernice shook her head and smiled.

"Unless some rich cookie maker leaves me a bunch of dough, I'll just have to leave the mansion to its ghosts," she said half-jokingly. "But now,

I've got to get back to the shop. Those dinosaur bones won't sell themselves!"

She winked, but it was clear that she didn't feel very jolly. The kids waved goodbye and went into Iggy's house.

"Did you really see a cat?" asked Ada, watching Iggy unfold the paper from his pocket and spread it out on the dining room table.

Iggy didn't answer.

He was too busy thinking.

Iggy wondered. Had he seen a cat? Or had he seen the paper blowing past? There were so many strange things at the mansion. Maybe he'd imagined it. But what about the cat on the porch during the storm? Had he imagined that, too? Iggy scowled. He spent a lot of time imagining buildings and bridges and other structures. But NOT cats!

Sofia smiled at her friend. She could always

tell when something bugged Iggy. She changed the subject.

"Speaking of cookies," she said, opening her messenger bag, "Abuelo baked us some!"

Sofia's grandfather had owned a bakery in their neighborhood for many years. La Panaderia de la Magnolia was the best bakery around. He was retired now, but he still baked for Sofia and her friends.

"My folks left some food for us, too," Iggy said.

He popped out of his chair and left the room. A moment later, he came back with a tray of food and glasses of lemonade.

"I've got questions!" said Ada Twist, reaching for some grapes.

"Me too!" said Sofia.

"Me three!" said Rosie.

Iggy said nothing. He was too busy thinking.

- What happened to Herbert Sherbert?
- Is the mansion haunted?
- Where is the furniture from the mansion?
- Why did his cat look just like Bricks?
- Are ghosts real?
- What made the porch go wacky and why did it stop?
- Will you pass the cheese?
- How could one lever open all the shutters at the same time?

What Why How

CHAPTER 13

Rosie pulled her notebook from her pocket and the pencil from behind her ear and took notes as they talked.

They chatted and chomped and made notes.

"What about Aunt Bernice?" asked Ada.

Rosie stopped writing and looked up at her friend. Ada frowned and tapped her chin.

"Aunt Bernice loves the house," said Ada. "But she doesn't have enough money to fix it up. We're going to help her keep it!"

"Let's make a machine to scare away the ghost!" said Rosie. "If there is a ghost. How can we tell if there's really a ghost?"

"We can do an experiment!" said Ada. "But what kind of experiment?"

She reached for another cookie. They were gone.

And so was Iggy.

They found Iggy in the kitchen. The refrigerator door and all the cabinets were flung open. Crackers, slices of bread, chunks of cheese, ice cream cones, and loose fruit were scattered over the floor.

"Zowie," said Ada.

Rising out of the mess was a model of the Mysterious Mansion.

"Looks beautiful!" said Rosie.

"Looks delicious," said Ada.

"It's all wrong," said Iggy.

"No, Iggy," said Sofia. "It looks amazing!"

Iggy looked at her oddly. Then he looked at the model and back at his friends.

"Oh," he said. "The model looks right. But the mansion is all wrong. We need to find out why, and I have an idea."

They cleaned up and made a plan. Then, they went outside. Sofia and Ada ran toward City Hall and the library. Rosie and Iggy ran to Rosie's house and climbed into the heli-o-cheese-copter.

"Fueled up and ready to fly!" said Rosie. "Helmets on!"

They buckled into the cockpit and Rosie hit the switch. The cheese-copter sputtered and twitched and off they flew! They zoomed past Iggy Peck Bridge to the woods. The Mysterious Mansion rose from the surrounding forest.

Iggy motioned for Rosie to circle the property. She hit the throttle and expertly flew around the mansion three times. From the air, they could see new details.

"Look at the
ornaments!" shouted
Iggy, pointing to the
fancy decorations on the
two giant chimneys that
rose from either end of
the mansion.

"Gargoyles!" he yelled,
pointing at the downspouts
shaped like faces.

"Can we go over the
top?" Iggy asked.

"Hold on!" yelled
Rosie.

She pulled back
on the throttle, and
the cheese-copter
zoomed up, up, up, and
over the midsection
of the mansion.

"Look!" yelled Iggy, pointing to the roof of the mansion.

The cheese-copter hovered over the roof.

"Yahoo!" yelled Iggy, pointing at the roof. "I knew it would be like that!"

Rosie grinned and nodded.

"You were right!" she said.

Iggy gave the thumbs-up sign, and Rosie Revere turned the cheese-copter toward City Hall.

CHAPTER 14

They landed with a THUMP on the grass next to Blue River Creek City Hall. Iggy and Rosie hopped out and sat down on the City Hall steps. Iggy pulled out his notebook and started sketching.

A few minutes later, Sofia called to them as she ran down the wide stone steps. She waved a handful of papers.

"Hey!" called Sofia. "Look what I found! Clerk Clark knew exactly where to look."

Sofia knew her way around City Hall. She had gone often when she was working to get a new park built in Blue River Creek. She'd made a lot of friends there, including Clara Clark, the city clerk.

"Look at these building permits for the mansion!" said Sofia. "The first one is from 1875. That's when they built the original house.

"The last one is from January 1918," she said. "They completely changed the inside to be Art Nouveau, and they added a whole new wing in that style."

"1918?" said Iggy. "That was the year on the gravestone."

"Were there permits after 1918?" asked Rosie.

"Nothing," said Sofia.

Just then, they saw Ada running toward them from the library. She was carrying a big book.

"Look!" said Ada. "I found a collection of society columns from Blue River Creek! Check out this article."

March 10, 1918

Blue River Creek was at its finest today as families came together to celebrate the seventh birthday of Miss Honey Sherbert. She is, of course, the daughter of Candace and Herbert Sherbert and heiress to their ice cream empire.

The town's citizens gathered on the lawn of the Sherbert Mansion for a day of picnics, songs, dances, and tours of the elegant mansion. Entertainment was provided by the traveling French acrobatic group, Le Flip.

A wonderful time was had by all. Next year's party is already being planned!

"That's why there's a Honey Festival in town every year?" Iggy said. "I thought it was just because people like bees!"

"I love bees," said Ada.

"What happened to Honey?" asked Sofia.

Ada flipped to a different page. A sad look crossed her face.

"It's awful," she said.

Flu Epidemic Returns

Blue River Creek has been struck by tragedy. The Spanish flu has claimed the life of Candace Sherbert, local leader in the women's suffrage movement and wife of ice cream creator Herbert Sherbert. Mr. and Mrs. Sherbert lost their only daughter, Honey, to the flu epidemic one month ago.

Mrs. Sherbert is the twentieth person in Blue River Creek to die from the Spanish Flu this year. The numbers are expected to rise as the flu spreads through the country. Officials warn that millions may perish worldwide due to the disease.

Iggy gasped.

"It was their graves in the forest!" he said. "H. Sherbert was Honey, not Herbert! I didn't know the flu was so dangerous."

"People can still die from the flu, but it's not as common," said Ada, "because scientists invented new medicines and vaccines. People used to die of all kinds of diseases like measles and flu. Vaccines changed that. Mr. McClintock at the library said that millions of people around the world died from flu in 1918. Millions!"

"Look at the article date," said Rosie. "It was just four months after the Honey Festival."

"What happened to Herbert after that?" asked Iggy.

"I don't know," said Ada. "I have to read more to find out. What did you and Rosie find, Iggy?"

"Something we need to show your great-aunt. Now!" said Iggy.

Things in the can you dig it? shop

 RocKs

 Dinosaur Bones

Old Jewelry

 Pottery

A Meteorite!

CHAPTER 15

The Questioneers ran toward the Can You Dig It? shop a block from City Hall. The shop was packed with everything you could dig from the ground. There were rocks, dinosaur bones, old jewelry, pottery, and a meteorite! There was even a worm farm in the corner. There were also books and papers and maps and hats and all kinds of historical things from Blue River Creek that Aunt Bernice had found as she researched the things she dug up.

"Aunt Bernice?" called Ada as they stepped into the shop.

"She's not here," said a woman with short red hair and a polka-dot scarf like the one Rosie wore. "I'm watching the shop while she's gone."

It was June, one of Aunt Bernice's best friends.

"When will she be back?" asked Rosie.

"Not until tomorrow," said June. "She's gone out of town with Agnes Lu. Oh, Bernice is so worried."

"Why?" asked Ada.

"That Mysterious Mansion, of course," said June. "She lost her heart to that place but it's going to cost a fortune to fix up. So she and Agnes took the Treasure to some experts to see how much it's worth. If it's worth enough, she can get a loan or sell some treasure to pay for repairs on the mansion."

Ada looked at the glass case where Aunt Bernice kept her most valuable items. She knew

the contents by heart: eleven golden rings, a cup filled with rare gems, silver antique spoons, a meteorite, six dinosaur bones, and a T. rex tooth. Aunt Bernice called them the Treasure.

Now, the case was empty.

"It's all happening so fast," said June. "Today, a lady offered to buy the mansion and needs an answer by tomorrow. If she doesn't get the mansion from Bernice, then she's going to buy some other property the next day. Bernice has to decide immediately to keep it or sell. That lady is making a great offer. It's a tough decision!"

"Who is she?" asked Iggy.

"Head over to your folks' gallery and find out!" said June. "She's there now!"

CHAPTER 16

Iggy's parents, Marcia Hunt and Fred Peck, helped people in Blue River Creek buy and sell property and art. Their gallery was around the corner from Aunt Bernice's shop.

The Questioneers ran to the Hunt and Peck Gallery and burst through the door. A short jolly woman was chatting happily with Iggy's parents.

"Iggy!" said his father. "This is Miss Weatherbee. She just put in an offer on the Sherbert House."

"But . . ." sputtered Iggy.

"You must be the young architect I've heard so much about," said Miss Weatherbee. "I think you'll love the new apartments I plan to build."

"But it belongs to Aunt Bernice," said Ada.

"Of course! She has to sell it first," said Miss Weatherbee cheerily. "I hope she does. Then I'll clear the land and knock down the current structures and build a wonderful, new, modern living community."

Iggy gasped.

"Do what?" he asked in disbelief.

Miss Weatherbee did not notice.

"Just imagine," she continued, "a ten-building apartment complex with each building looking just like the others! It will be something to see!"

Iggy's eyes got wide. His mouth fell open, but no sound came out. His face turned bright red and the room began to spin.

"I think he's going to faint!" said Ada. "Sit down, Iggy!"

"Oh my. Does he always do that?" asked Miss Weatherbee. "Well, I'll see you all at the Sherbert place tomorrow."

She waved cheerily and left the gallery.

"Good gracious, Ignatius," said Iggy's mom. "Are you all right?"

"She can't tear down the mansion!" said Iggy. "Think of the marble floors! Think of the iron staircase! Think of the gargoyles!"

"Hopefully Bernice will be able to keep it," said Mr. Peck. "We'll know more tomorrow."

"Iggy, you go home and take it easy," said Iggy's mother. "That was a pretty big shock."

The Questioneers headed back to the heli-o-cheese-copter. They sat down on the grass.

"Are you feeling any better?" asked Sofia.

"No," said Iggy. "She's going to tear down the mansion!"

"I know that's scary for you," said Sofia.

They sat silently for a moment. Suddenly, Iggy jumped up.

"That's it!" he said.

"What's it?" asked Sofia.

"Scary!" said Iggy. "It's so SCARY!"

He grinned.

"I don't get it," said Ada.

"Boooooooooo!" said Iggy.

He waited a moment. Then, one by one, they got it.

"Oh my," said Sofia.

"Oh my," said Rosie.

"Zowie!" said Ada.

CHAPTER 17

The next afternoon, Iggy and his parents stood on the front porch of the Sherbert Mansion with Miss Weatherbee. Iggy listened nervously as she pointed at the forest.

"If we take out those trees," she said, "I could add three more apartment buildings! All in a perfect line!"

Iggy groaned. How could anyone want to knock down an architectural masterpiece like the Mysterious Mansion?

"But we need this place! It's important," said Iggy. "Architecture is important! It lets us show who we are. It lets us show where we've been and lets us decide where we want to go! Architecture is one way we show the world what's important to us! We can't just tear down old places like this. We need them!"

"Oh my," said Miss Weatherbee. "That is an interesting view. But just imagine having lots and lots of nice simple places for people to live. Nice square places. That sounds so neat and tidy."

Iggy felt woozy and was about to plop onto the steps when he heard the sound.

BEEP! BEEP!

An old military jeep zoomed up the driveway.

BEEP! BEEP!

It was Aunt Bernice and Agnes Lu.

"They're here!" yelled Iggy.

His excitement faded when he saw the grim expressions on their faces. Aunt Bernice had not found the money to keep the Mysterious Mansion.

"Hello, Miss Weatherbee," said Aunt Bernice, climbing the steps to the porch. "Hi, Fred. Hi, Marcia."

"Any luck?" asked Iggy's mom.

"Not enough. I guess I won't be keeping this marvelous place," said Aunt Bernice. "Let's sign the sales contract and be done."

"But wait!" said Iggy. "We should go inside!"

"No point, Iggy," said Aunt Bernice. "Plus, I don't have a key. Remember? My keys didn't open the door."

"But . . ." Iggy started.

"But what?" asked Mrs. Lu.

Iggy scooted toward the door.

"BUT WHAT ABOUT *THE GHOSTS*?" he said in a *very* loud voice.

"Oh my," said Miss Weatherbee. "I'm not a fan of ghosts."

"They're awful!" said Iggy. "GHOSTS ARE A REAL PROBLEM AROUND HERE!"

"Why are you yelling?" asked Iggy's father.

"JUST KEEPING AWAY THE GHOSTS!" yelled Iggy. "DON'T WANT ANY OF *THOSE* TO SHOW UP!"

"Ignatius," said Iggy's mother, "are you feeling okay?"

"Ghosts can show up anytime," said Iggy. "ANY TIME AT ALL!"

Suddenly . . .

BUMP! THUMP! BUMP! THUMP!

"What's going on?" cried Miss Weatherbee. "There's something wrong with the porch!"

The boards of the porch bounced up and down.

BUMP! THUMP! BUMP! THUMP!

"It's the ghost of Herbert Sherbert!" said Iggy in his spookiest voice. "He's back!"

WHOMP!

The porch boards slammed down.

Then . . .

CRRRREEEEEAAAK!

The mansion door swung open.

"WHOOOOOOOOO! WHOOOOOOOOOOOOO!"

A wailing cry came from the darkness inside.

"The ghost!" said Iggy.

A deep rumbling noise rose from the house, and suddenly, there was music. Loud, creepy circus music filled the air.

"Whooooooo! WHOOOOOOOOOO!"

The willowy, wavy ghost of Herbert Sherbert appeared in the light of the doorway for an instant.

And then it was gone.

"A ghost!" yelled Iggy. "It's haunted! Nobody would rent apartments here!"

"AHEM!"

Aunt Bernice cleared her throat loudly and gave Iggy a very stern look.

"What's going on?" she asked.

Iggy waved his hands in the air.

"It's the ghost of Herbert Sherbert!" he said. "Whoooooo! He's back and he doesn't like apartment buildings!"

"We shall see," said Aunt Bernice, heading through the door.

As she stepped into the Great Hall, the music stopped. Once more, the ghostly howl began again.

"WHOOOOOOOOOOOOOOOOOOOOOOOOOOO! WHOOOOOOOOO-WHOOOOOOOOOOOOOOO!"

Aunt Bernice pulled the lever on the wall.

BAM! BAM! BAM!

The metal shutters flipped open and light streamed into the Great Hall and onto the ghost of Herbert Sherbert.

CHAPTER 18

The ghost of Herbert Sherbert stood on the swirling marble floor with its six feet sticking out from beneath its enormous white body.

"Whoooooooooooooo . . ."

"Excuse me," said Iggy's father. "We can see your shoes."

"Oops," said the ghost, pulling its feet under the sheet.

"I'm the ghost of Herbert Sherbert!" said the ghost. "Whoooooooooo!"

"You look like a giant white spider," said Iggy's mother.

"Spiders have eight legs!" said the ghost.

There were whispers beneath the sheet.

". . . Ghosts don't care . . . They would if they studied spiders . . . Shhhh . . ."

Aunt Bernice pulled away the sheet to reveal Rosie, Ada, and Sofia holding sticks to lift up the sheet.

"Well?" said Aunt Bernice. "What do you have to say?"

"Boo?" asked Ada.

"I'm so confused!" said Miss Weatherbee. "Are there ghosts? Or not? I don't like ghosts! They are terrible for house sales."

"It's just us," said Ada. "We were trying to help, but maybe we didn't."

"We wanted to scare you away so you wouldn't tear down this beautiful place!" said Iggy. "It is an important example of Art Nouveau architecture and Victorian architecture—"

"And Blue River Creek history—" said Sofia.

"I know you meant well," Aunt Bernice said kindly, "but this is not how we do things. I only want this place if I can keep it fair and square."

"What is going on?" said Iggy's mother.

The kids began talking all at once.

". . . ghosts . . . porch gears . . . experiment . . . keyhole switch . . . portrait . . . Herbert? . . . BOO! . . . architecture . . . gargoyle . . . library . . . booger . . . blueprints . . ."

Aunt Bernice laughed and raised her hand.

"One at a time," she said.

Rosie jumped in.

"Yesterday, I saw gears under the porch boards," she said. "So I figured the moving porch wasn't a ghost. It was just a gizmo! The porch went crazy when we put the wrong key in the lock. When we moved the crooked portrait, the house started making sounds. I figured out those were switches. Herbert Sherbert was a great engineer, and he rigged the house to act like it was haunted."

"Like a booby trap?" asked Miss Weatherbee. "Why would he do that?"

"His heart broke when his family died," said Ada. "Maybe he didn't want strangers living in the house, so he scared away people who tried to get in."

"Like you said, Miss Weatherbee," said Iggy, "ghosts are bad for house sales. If that was Herbert Sherbert's plan, it worked! It kept people from trying to buy the house."

Miss Weatherbee nodded.

"How did you kids get in today?" asked Aunt Bernice. "Bee and Beau boarded up the window yesterday."

"I invented a gadget," said Rosie. "It's the Keypopper 7!"

She held up a contraption with a bunch of weird spikes sticking out of it.

"This part opens the door," said Rosie. "This part trips the booby traps! You can keep it for when you live here."

"You are all so clever," said Aunt Bernice. "But I have to sell the place."

"What about the antiques?" asked Ada.

"Oh, my dear," said Aunt Bernice. "We can't even guess what was here so long ago."

"But we can!" said Sofia. "Just look!"

She pulled the library book from her satchel and flipped through the pages.

"Here!" she said.

Sofia held up a photograph of Mrs. Candace Sherbert and another woman standing in the Great Hall of the mansion—and the hall was full of expensive-looking furniture and antiques! Sofia read the photograph's caption. "January 12, 1916. Candace Sherbert hosted Ida B. Wells in the Great Hall. Ida B. Wells is a leader in the fight for women's suffrage in America. Suffragists, like

Candace Sherbert and Ida B. Wells, believe that women should have the right to vote. 'Ice cream for kids,' said Mrs. Sherbert. 'Votes for women!'"

"That is history!" said Aunt Bernice. "And look at all that furniture! But it's all gone now. We've searched everywhere."

"There's one place we didn't look!" said Iggy.

He took out his sketch of the mansion roof.

"This is what we saw from the cheese-copter," he said.

"There must be a hidden room!" said Ada. "Maybe this key from the lawyers opens the door to the secret space!"

She held up the ribbon with the key.

"But where is this room?" asked Aunt Bernice.

Iggy held up his drawing.

"Here!" he said.

Glass dome

△

Iron and glass

CHAPTER 19

Iggy's hand-drawn blueprint showed the rooms they had visited. He pointed to a blank area in the middle of the second floor.

"Architects don't leave blank parts in a house," he said. "It has to be a secret room!"

They followed the blueprint to a second-floor hallway with many bedroom doorways to the right, but no doors to the left.

"The bedrooms on the right have windows to

the yard," said Ada. "So, the secret room has to be on the left wall."

"But where?" asked Sofia.

There were eight panels along the hallway. The panels were covered with complicated Art Nouveau wallpaper with hundreds of flowers and ice cream cones.

"That's a lot of ice cream cones," said Miss Weatherbee.

The kids spread out and searched for a keyhole, a switch, or a button. Anything that would open a hidden door. They found nothing.

Sofia sat down and looked at the library book.

"Let's face it," said Aunt Bernice. "The furniture is long gone."

"Do you think the caretaker took it?" asked Ada.

"Oh, no," said Aunt Bernice. "Monsieur Glace

was a kind old man. He lived in the little cottage and gave candy to everyone he met."

"I remember him!" said Iggy's father. "He had a little beard and a green cap and he always looked exactly the same."

"He did! I don't think he ever changed," said Aunt Bernice. "And he always said the same thing . . ."

"'Happiness is the key to everything!'" said Aunt Bernice and Iggy's father at the same time.

They laughed.

"Why did he always look the same?" asked Ada.

"I don't know," said Iggy's dad. "He just always did."

Just then, Sofia popped up and ran to the others.

"Aha!" she cried. "Look at this one!"

She showed them another article.

October 7, 1918

It is a sad day in Blue River Creek. Our most famous citizen, Herbert Sherbert, creator of Green Goose ice cream, bids farewell to our fair city. Following the tragic loss of his beloved wife, Candace, and his daughter, Honey, he is returning to France. He leaves behind a grateful town and many happy customers.

His seventy-year-old cousin, Pierre Glace, will act as caretaker to the Sherbert House and estate. He will arrive tomorrow on the three o'clock train.

The group studied the photo.

"Why would he have such a small suitcase for such a long trip?" asked Miss Weatherbee.

"Why would he go to France in 1918?" asked Agnes Lu. "The First World War was going on! That would be dangerous!"

"Why did Pierre Glace arrive after Herbert left?" asked Iggy's mother. "Wouldn't he want to see his cousin?"

"Doesn't *glace* mean 'ice cream' in French?" asked Aunt Bernice.

"How could Pierre Glace be seventy when he got here in 1918 and still be alive fifty years later? And look the same?" asked Iggy's father.

"Look at us!" said Aunt Bernice. "We're all becoming Questioneers!"

Everyone laughed.

Everyone but Iggy.

Iggy looked sadly at the picture for a moment. Then he asked a simple question.

"Where is his cat?" he asked.

CHAPTER 20

I'd never leave Bricks if I moved to France," said Iggy.

Rosie looked worried.

"What if—" she started.

Iggy knew what she was going to say. He thought about the cat statues near the old cottage. Were they statues? Or were they gravestones?

He tried to remember the words on the statues. What were they? Whimsy and Wonder and—

His thoughts were interrupted by Agnes Lu.

"Bernice," she said. "Herbert Sherbert wanted someone like you to have his house. Wouldn't he leave a clue about the secret room?"

Whimsy and Wonder and what was it?

"I am confused about everything," said Miss Weatherbee.

As the word *everything* left her mouth, a different word entered Iggy's brain.

HAPPINESS!

"Happiness!" he yelled. "Whimsy and Wonder and Happiness!"

The group looked at him oddly.

"Happiness!" he said jumping up and down. "The key to EVERYTHING is HAPPINESS!"

"What?" asked Ada.

"Herbert Sherbert left a clue!" said Iggy.

"Where?" asked Aunt Bernice.

"EVERYWHERE!" said Iggy. "Don't you see? Happiness is the key to everything."

"We know," said Rosie. "That's his slogan."

"No," said Iggy. "Happiness was his cat! Its grave is by the cottage."

"Oh my," said Aunt Bernice. "Herbert Sherbert put that message on buildings all around town! In the original library and the train station!"

"The important buildings where everybody would see it," said Iggy. "And as part of the architecture."

"And his cousin said that to everyone!" said Ada.

"Wait a minute!" said Sofia. "What if he wasn't?"

"Wasn't what?" asked Ada.

"What if Pierre Glace wasn't Herbert Sherbert's cousin?" Sofia said. "What if he was Herbert Sherbert?

"Think about it!" she continued. "What if Herbert Sherbert took a train from Blue River Creek one day and came back the next day in a disguise? He pretended not to speak much English so people wouldn't hear his voice."

"Except when he passed along the clue," said Iggy's father.

"Why did he hide the furniture?" asked Ada.

"To keep away thieves," said Miss Weatherbee. "A house full of expensive furniture and art from around the world would be quite a prize for thieves."

Aunt Bernice put her hand to her mouth.

"Poor lonely soul," she said. "He scared everyone away to protect the memory of his family. I can imagine him sitting in that chair by the portrait all alone."

"I don't think he was alone," said Iggy. "I think he had a cat."

CHAPTER 21

I saw three cat statues by the cottage," Iggy said. "Happiness wasn't the only one. So maybe he always had cats."

"If his cat was Happiness," said Ada, "what did the clue mean?"

They stepped into the Thailand room and looked at the mural. The white cat stared back at them.

Iggy stared at the cat's odd eyes. What was it trying to tell them?

The green gemstones on the cat's painted collar seemed to sparkle in the afternoon light.

Sofia looked closer at the collar.

"That's so beautiful," she said. "The green gems are sitting on tiny ice cream cones. Maybe one of the green ice cream cones in the house is a switch, too!"

Aunt Bernice groaned.

"That's no help at all," she said. "There are a thousand little green ice cream cones on the walls and floors and ceilings of this house. We could spend years testing them all."

They walked back to the hall.

Iggy looked at his blueprint and at the hallway lined with panels.

"It has to be here somewhere," he said.

Iggy looked around. He frowned. He thought. Then he thought some more.

"What did Clerk Clark say about the building permits?" he asked.

"She said the last updates on the house were done here in 1918," said Sofia.

"A few months before Candace and Honey Sherbert died," said Ada.

"Someone did work after that!" Iggy said. "Look!"

Iggy pointed to the panel of wallpaper behind Aunt Bernice.

"It's ice cream, Iggy," she said. "Just like the other panels."

"No!" said Iggy. "It's different."

The pattern was complicated and filled with colored ice cream cones like the other panels. But it had sharp angles instead of winding curves. It was sleek and modern.

"It's Art Deco!" said Iggy's father.

"Good gracious, Ignatius," said his mother. "It is!"

"So?" asked Sofia.

"So," said Iggy's mom, "Art Deco was introduced to the world in 1925 in Paris. It wouldn't be on wallpaper before then."

"So?" asked Rosie.

"So," said Iggy, "this panel is newer than the others. Somebody put this wallpaper up after 1925! The door has to be behind this one!"

"Is there a green ice cream cone?" asked Ada. "Like on the cat's collar?"

The tiny ice cream cones covered the panel. There was chocolate, strawberry, vanilla, lemon, orange, and green ones. They were covered with multicolored sprinkles.

"They're everywhere," said Iggy. "It's not the ans—"

"Wait!" yelled Sofia. "Look at that cone!"

She pointed to a vanilla cone near the top. It was different from the others.

Instead of white ice cream with green sprinkles, the cone contained one beautiful white Art Deco cat with a green-jeweled collar.

"That's it!" said Iggy. "That's got to be it!"

Ada handed the key to Aunt Bernice, who pushed it through the green spot on the cat's collar with a *SNAP!*

"It's a keyhole!" said Aunt Bernice.

She turned the key.

SNAP! CLICK!

The panel swung open.

"Zowie!" said Ada.

"You can say that again," said Aunt Bernice.

"Zowie," said the Questioneers.

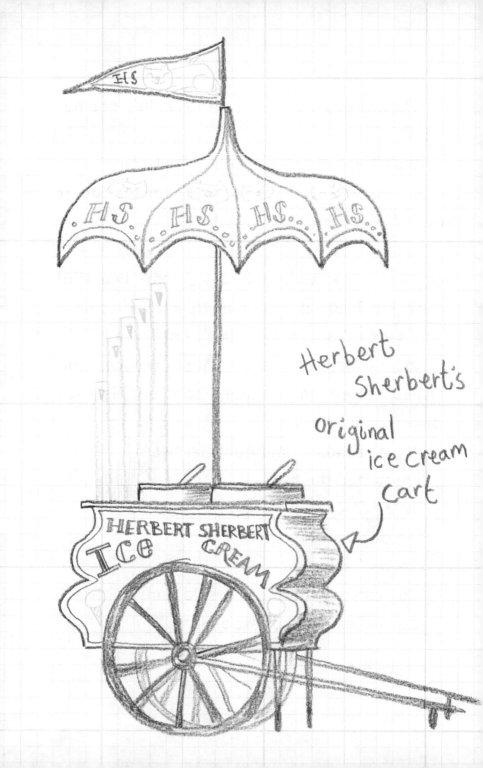

Herbert Sherbert's

original ice cream cart

CHAPTER 22

The room was filled from floor to glass ceiling with stacks of chairs, tables, bedframes, mirrors, paintings, dishes, and statues. Everything needed to furnish a mansion. In one corner stood a strange, brightly painted organ with long copper pipes. It was Herbert Sherbert's original ice cream cart. The invention that started it all.

An iron and glass ceiling arched over the entire space. Only a few panes of glass were missing in the ceiling. A stack of wooden crates beneath

one of the missing panes showed signs of water
damage.

They looked around in awe.

"Look, Aunt Bernice!" said Ada.

A handwritten note sat on a small table.

Welcome, My Friend,

At last, you are here. Did you have help? We all have help, if we are lucky. I was a very lucky man, indeed. My life was full of love.

When my loves left, I shut out the world. I did not want it here, melting away my memories like ice cream in the sun. Perhaps I was foolish. Time does not stop because we wish it to.

I do not know when you arrived, but if you have found this note, the time is right for the house to find a new life. Once, this house echoed with laughter and joy. I hope that it will do so again for you. Though it has been silent for so many years, the love that dwelled within these walls still remains.

Never forget: Happiness is the key to everything!

Welcome home.

Herbert "Pierre Glace" Sherbert

Meeooooooo

The Ghost Cat

CHAPTER 23

Aunt Bernice wiped a tear from her eye.

"I had so much help," she said, looking at Iggy, Ada, Rosie, and Sofia.

"And I have an idea," she said. "I know how to fill this place with laughter again, just like Herbert Sherbert wanted."

"So, you're keeping the mansion?" asked Miss Weatherbee.

Aunt Bernice nodded.

"I don't blame you," said Miss Weatherbee.

"It's *almost* as great as ten perfectly square apartment buildings. And I'm glad there aren't any ghosts!"

Suddenly, a deep rumble rose from the organ. A loud note erupted from the pipe. Then another note, and another. The keys of the organ popped up and down all by themselves.

Miss Weatherbee jumped a foot off the floor.

"Eeek!" she cried.

Aunt Bernice and Iggy's parents scowled.

"Iggy?" said his father, tapping his toe on the ground.

"It's not me!" said Iggy.

"We're not doing it!" said Ada and Rosie.

"Then who is?" asked Aunt Bernice.

"It's the ghost!" said Miss Weatherbee. "Enjoy your mansion, Mrs. Twist. Goodbye!"

Miss Weatherbee ran from the room, down the stairs, and out the front door of the Mysterious Mansion. A moment later, the Questioneers heard the squealing of tires on the driveway as she sped away.

They looked at one another with wide eyes.

The organ played faster and louder. Then, suddenly, it stopped. There was silence. Then, something rattled behind the organ. Iggy gulped and took a step toward it.

Iggy stepped closer.

And closer.

And—

He dived behind the organ.

CRASH!

SMASH!

YEOOOOWWWWWW!

A bloodcurdling yowl filled the air, like the sound of a woman's scream.

The group gasped. Then suddenly, out stepped Iggy Peck holding a white cat with two different-colored eyes. Iggy was followed by a parade of kittens.

"Meet the Ghost Cat!" said Iggy. "And family."

"She must climb in and out of that missing windowpane up there," said Rosie.

"I'll have to fix that glass," said Aunt Bernice. "And get a new roof. And new wiring. And fix the kitchen window, and . . ."

This time, Aunt Bernice smiled as she listed off the repairs the Mysterious Mansion needed.

"And," she said, "I'll have to buy cat food, too! I wonder what a Ghost Cat and her kittens eat."

CHAPTER 24

Come one, come all!

The New Blue River Creek Honey Festival

Picnic on the lawn!
Ice cream and dancing for all!

ggy Peck stood next to Aunt Bernice on the porch of the Mysterious Mansion. A few weeks before, the house had been empty. Now, all of Blue River Creek was there, picnicking on the lawn. The sounds of music and laughter filled the air.

Iggy looked into the Great Hall at the picnic mural of Honey Sherbert's birthday party. He looked back at the yard. It was as if history had repeated itself.

Iggy smiled at Aunt Bernice.

"I think Herbert and Candace Sherbert would have liked this," said Iggy.

"Me too," said Aunt Bernice.

She nodded toward the portrait of Herbert and Candace Sherbert.

Iggy blinked and looked again. The portrait looked different. Something small but important had changed, but what was it? Herbert stood next to his bride, Candace, with her bouquet of jasmine and her white cat.

Iggy stared for a moment, trying to figure out what had changed. At last he knew. It was their eyes.

The sorrow in their eyes was gone. It was replaced by joy.

"How—?" Iggy started.

"I don't know," said Aunt Bernice.

Just then, Ada, Rosie, and Sofia ran into the Great Hall. They hugged Aunt Bernice and laughed.

"Welcome home!" they said.

"Thank you," Aunt Bernice said, hugging them back. "Thank you all."

The Questioneers ran out of the house and joined the dance party on the lawn. The McCallister Sisters were starting a set of favorite tunes.

Aunt Bernice followed the kids to the doorway. She paused for a heartbeat and looked once more at the portrait.

"Thank you," she whispered.

She smiled as a slight breeze stirred, carrying with it the faint, sweet scent of jasmine.

ODE TO AN ARCHITECT

Architect, architect. What do you see?
I look at a space and see what might be.

Architect, architect. What do you do?
I take an idea and make it come true.

ART NOUVEAU AND ART DECO

Styles of architecture develop for many reasons. New materials and tools let architects explore shapes and sizes of structures. Politics, historical events, and the arts influence how people think about themselves and the buildings they make. Sometimes people just want something different. New styles emerge.

In Europe and America, the nineteenth century (1800–1900) began with architects looking back to ancient Greece and Rome for inspiration. In the middle of the 1800s, there was a boom of new machines and inventions using powerful energy sources like steam and coal. This led to cast iron, and stronger steel and glass. Buildings got bigger and taller as a result. Glass and metal could also be used as ornamentation.

Art Nouveau means "new art" in French. Instead of looking back to the formal styles of

Greek and Roman architecture, Art Nouveau looked to nature for shapes and designs. It used curving iron frames filled with glass. Many images were based on leaves and flowers. Art Nouveau style was found in designs of furniture, posters, books, stained glass lamps, jewelry, and many other objects. This style was very popular from about 1890 until about 1920.

Art Deco was a style that became famous in 1925 because of an international show in Paris for the decorative and modern industrial arts. At that time, skyscrapers were springing up in America. Art Deco style looked to the future with sleek lines and geometric shapes. It was streamlined and elegant. One of the most famous examples of Art Deco architecture is the Chrysler Building in New York City, built in 1928. Art Deco was seen in furniture, murals, jewelry, fabric, and statues.

Weird, Wonderful, and Wonderfully Weird Cats
by Dr. Penelope H. Dee, PhD

Cats are weird. They stare at you when you are sleeping. They chase their own tails. They rumble when you pet them. They act like they want to go out when they are in and in when they are out. They are also wonderful and come in many different breeds.

One rare breed is the Khao Manee, which originated in Thailand hundreds of years ago. It was kept by royalty and is sometimes called a Diamond Eye cat. Khao Manee cats have pure-white coats that are smooth and short. They can have golden eyes or blue eyes. Sometimes, they have one of each! This is called "odd-eyed."

Here is how that happens. Pigment is a material that absorbs light and changes the color of the light it reflects back. Melanin is a kind of pigment found in animal tissue. The color of an animal's skin or eyes depends on the amount of melanin it has. The iris is the part of the eye that has color. If one of a cat's eyes does not have melanin, it will stay light blue. If the other eye does have melanin, it will become darker. Eyes with melanin can be gold, brown, or green. This trait of having different-colored eyes is called heterochromia. Heterochromia is usually genetic. That means it is passed from parents to their kittens. Each kitten of an odd-eyed cat has a one-in-two chance of having odd eyes.

HOW TO MAKE ICE CREAM

Have you ever heard anyone say, "I scream, you scream, we all scream for ice cream?"

Well, they were wrong. There is no need to scream for ice cream. You can simply make it yourself. It's very easy.

Here's what you need:

- 1 small zip-top bag (pint-size)
- 1 large zip-top bag (gallon-size)
- 1 cup of half-and-half (or $\frac{1}{2}$ cup whole milk and $\frac{1}{2}$ cup heavy cream)
- 2 tablespoons sugar
- $\frac{1}{2}$ teaspoon vanilla extract
- 4 cups ice cubes
- $\frac{1}{2}$ cup of kosher salt
- Dance music

Directions:

1. Pour sugar, vanilla, and half-and-half into small zip-top bag.

2. Seal the small bag.

3. Fill the large zip-top bag halfway with ice cubes.

4. Add kosher salt to the ice cubes.

5. Put small bag into the large bag.

6. Seal the large bag.

7. Dance to music for five to ten minutes while shaking the large bag. You can also sing while doing this, but singing will not speed up the freezing. It is, however, fun.

8. From time to time, squeeze the bags to see if the ice cream mix is the texture you like. When it is, simply open the big bag and

take out the little bag. You can add fruit, sprinkles, or whatever you like to your ice cream.

Congratulations, you made ice cream! Perhaps you will become a famous ice cream baron like Herbert Sherbert, who invented Green Goose ice cream. What will you name your flavor?

WHAT HAPPENED THERE?

The story of ice cream is all about freezing water! Each molecule of water has one atom of oxygen and two atoms of hydrogen (H_2O). These three atoms are bonded together loosely. Their bonds break and re-form all the time. But when the temperature drops to zero degrees Celsius (32 degrees Fahrenheit), the bonds hold strong and the water molecules arrange themselves in a shape with six sides called a lattice. The lattice is what makes up an ice crystal. You have probably seen ice crystals on a frosty windowpane in the winter.

The half-and-half you put into the small plastic bag contains a few things: water, milk fat globules, milk proteins, and sugar. To turn that mixture into ice cream, the water must form ice crystals. Here's the problem. The fat globules and other things in the mixture prevent ice crystals from forming at zero degrees Celsius. The mixture must get much colder for crystals to form.

But how can that happen? This is where the salt comes in. Salt lowers (or depresses) the temperature at which the ice crystals form. When salt is added to existing ice, it melts the ice and absorbs heat from whatever it is touching. In this case, the melting ice is touching the plastic bag with the half-and-half mixture. The warmth of the mixture is transferred to the melting ice. The temperature of the mixture goes down, down, down. Eventually, the water molecules in the mixture freeze and form ice crystals. THIS is when the mixture becomes ice cream!

The size of the ice crystals affects how creamy and smooth the ice cream will be. The smaller the crystals, the creamier the ice cream will be. Squishing the plastic bag and jumping up and down will help keep the ice crystals small.

People sometimes make ice cream in machines and churns, which add air bubbles to the ice cream and make it fluffy and light. Making ice cream is a science and an art. Have fun creating your own recipes and methods for the perfect ice cream!

WHO IS IDA B. WELLS?

In front of Blue River Creek City Hall, there stands a statue of a very brave woman. She holds a flag with a single word: *Truth*. This is a statue of Ida B. Wells.

Ida Bell Wells was an American journalist. She was a champion of justice for African Americans and for the rights of all women to vote. The right to vote in political elections is called *suffrage*. Those who fought for women's suffrage were called *suffragists* or sometimes called *suffragettes*.

Ida was born a slave in Mississippi on July 16, 1862, during the Civil War. Four months later, the Emancipation Proclamation freed slaves in the Confederate states. Her mother, who was a cook, and her father, who was a carpenter, worked to provide education to the freed slaves through Rust College.

When Ida was sixteen, yellow fever killed her parents and her baby brother. Ida wanted to keep the rest of her siblings together, so she dressed up like an eighteen-year-old and found a job as a teacher. Eventually, she moved her family to Memphis, Tennessee, and continued to teach. She also became a journalist and the owner of a Memphis newspaper called the *Free Speech and Headlight*.

Ida reported on violence toward African Americans by white mobs in the South. She also wrote about social injustice, especially in education where white students had better schools and supplies than black students. Some people did not like her writings, and she was fired as a teacher. In 1892, an angry white mob destroyed her newspaper office and threatened her life. She left Tennessee and eventually ended up in Chicago, Illinois. There, she married a man named Frederick Barnett and had four children. She never quit writing about the problems she saw.

She spent her life fighting against injustice and fighting for the rights of African Americans and all people. As a suffragist, she worked for women's voting rights and campaigned against the racial bigotry that even existed within the women's suffrage movement. American women gained the right to vote on August 26, 1920, with the ratification of the Nineteenth Amendment to the U.S. Constitution. Ida spent the rest of her life working for justice and truth.

Ida B. Wells died on March 25, 1931. In her life, she helped so many people in so many ways. She did so by spreading the truth, even when others did not want to hear it. As she once said, "The way to right wrongs is to turn the light of truth upon them."